Love You, Mouse Toy

Written by:
Flounder ~~Cat~~ M. Leipold
Fish

Love You, Mouse Toy

Copyright ©2025 Nina Leipold

www.FlounderCat.com

All rights reserved. No part of this publication may be reproduced, distributed, stored in a retrieval system, or transmitted, in any form or by any means, including electronic, mechanical, photocopying, recording or otherwise, without the prior written permission of the publisher, except in the case of brief quotations embodied in critical reviews, and certain other non-commercial uses permitted by copyright law.

Love You, Mouse Toy

for every animal ever dismissed or mistreated because their minds and hearts were not seen.

AnD mouse Toy

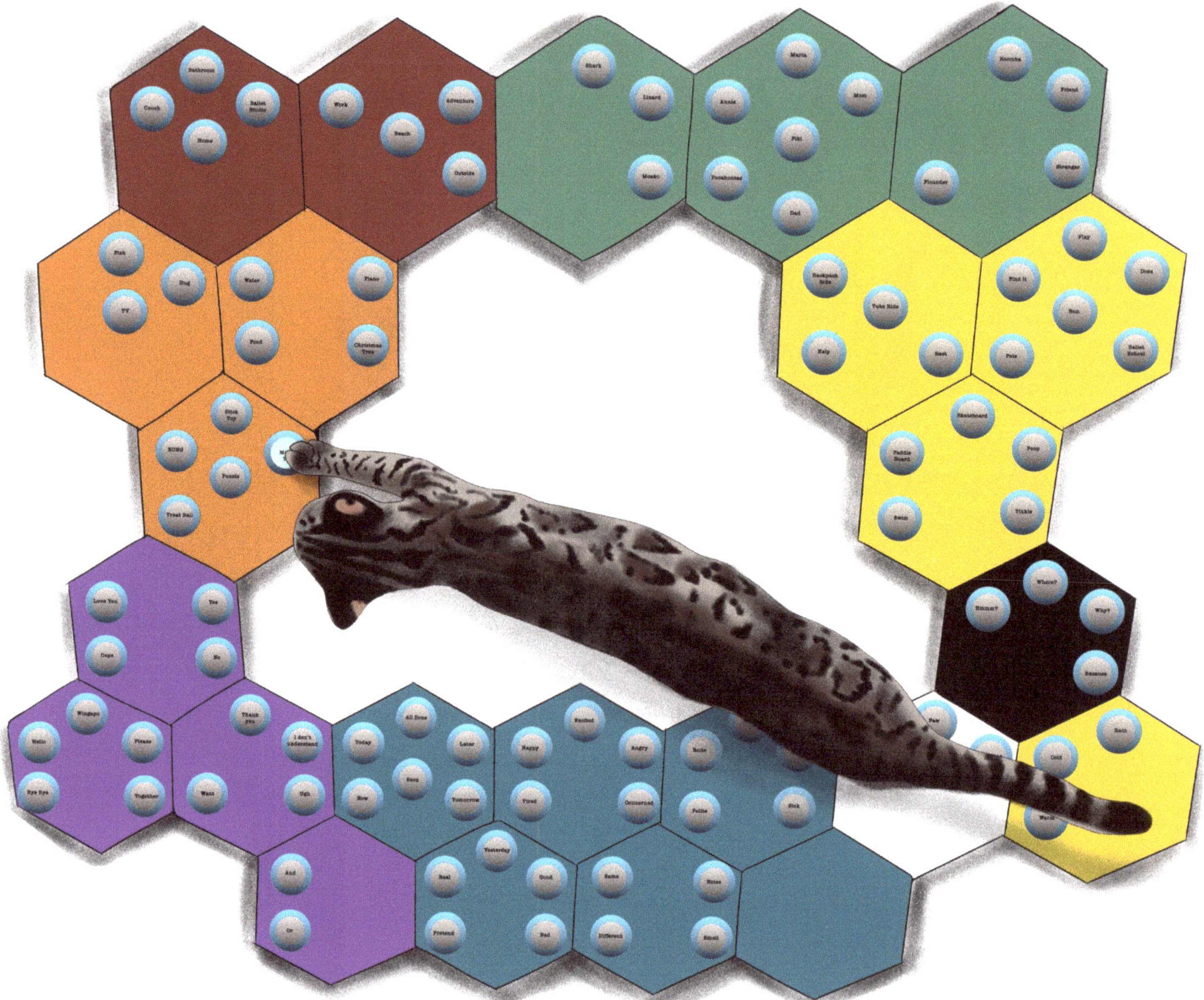

Bathroom
Couch
Ballet Studio
Home
Work
Adventure
Beach
Outside
Shark
Lizard
Marta
Annie
Mom
Pocahontas
Dad
Roomba
Friend
Flounder
Stranger
Fish
Dog
TV
Water
Piano
Food
Christmas Tree
Stick Toy
KONG
Puzzle
Treat Ball
Backpack Ride
Tube Ride
Help
Play
Find It
Done
Run
Ballet School
Skateboard
Paddle Board
Poop
Swim
Tinkle
Where?
Why?
Because
Love You
Yes
Oops
No
Hello
Please
Together
Thank you
I don't understand
Want
Ugh
All Done
Today
Later
Now
Soon
Tomorrow
Excited
Happy
Angry
Tired
Concerned
Smile
Sick
Yesterday
Good
Bad
Pretend
Same
Different
Noise
Smell
And
Or
Cold
Rain
Warm
Paw

Preface

My name is Nina, and my bestic is Flounder. Flounder is not just any cat (she calls herself a "fish")—she is a talking cat. She learned to use special buttons that let her share her thoughts, her wishes, and even her stories with me. Every word you read in this book (minus the context blurbs) is truly hers, pressed out one paw-tap at a time.

This is Flounder's very first book, and it is about someone very special to her—her beloved Mouse Toy. Mouse Toy is her best friend, her adventure buddy, and the star of many of her stories. You could say Mouse Toy lives in her heart and in her imagination all at once.

I helped her gather her words and put them on these pages, but the story is all hers. You are about to step into Flounder's world and see life through the eyes of a cat (fish) who finally found her voice. There is a QR code on each page so you can watch the video of her pressing the words on each page.

So curl up somewhere cozy, just like a cat would, and join Flounder as she tells you all about Mouse Toy—the friend who makes her whiskers twitch with happiness.

Happy Beach Mouse Toy

Mouse Toy enjoys going on adventures to the beach with Flounder. That makes him happy.

1

Mouse Toy Puzzle

Mouse Toy Treat Ball

Fish Mouse Toy

Tired Tomorrow Mouse Toy

After a big day of fun, all planned by Flounder, Mouse Toy was very tired the next day.

Mouse Toy Rest

Mouse Toy Ouch Does Pets

Mouse Toy got hurt one day
when he was playing with Flounder.
Flounder gave him pets
to make him feel better, but his ouch
would make him look a little bit different
from now on, and both Mouse Toy
and Flounder were fine with that.

Mouse Toy Happy Belly

After Mouse Toy got his
boo boo, Flounder fed him
her brother's food.
This made his belly happy.

Does Mouse Toy Mouse Toy Food?

Food Flounder Today
All Done Mouse Toy

Flounder checked with her mom to make sure she didn't feed Mouse Toy today. Then, Flounder fed Mouse Toy. She continues to feed him once a day.

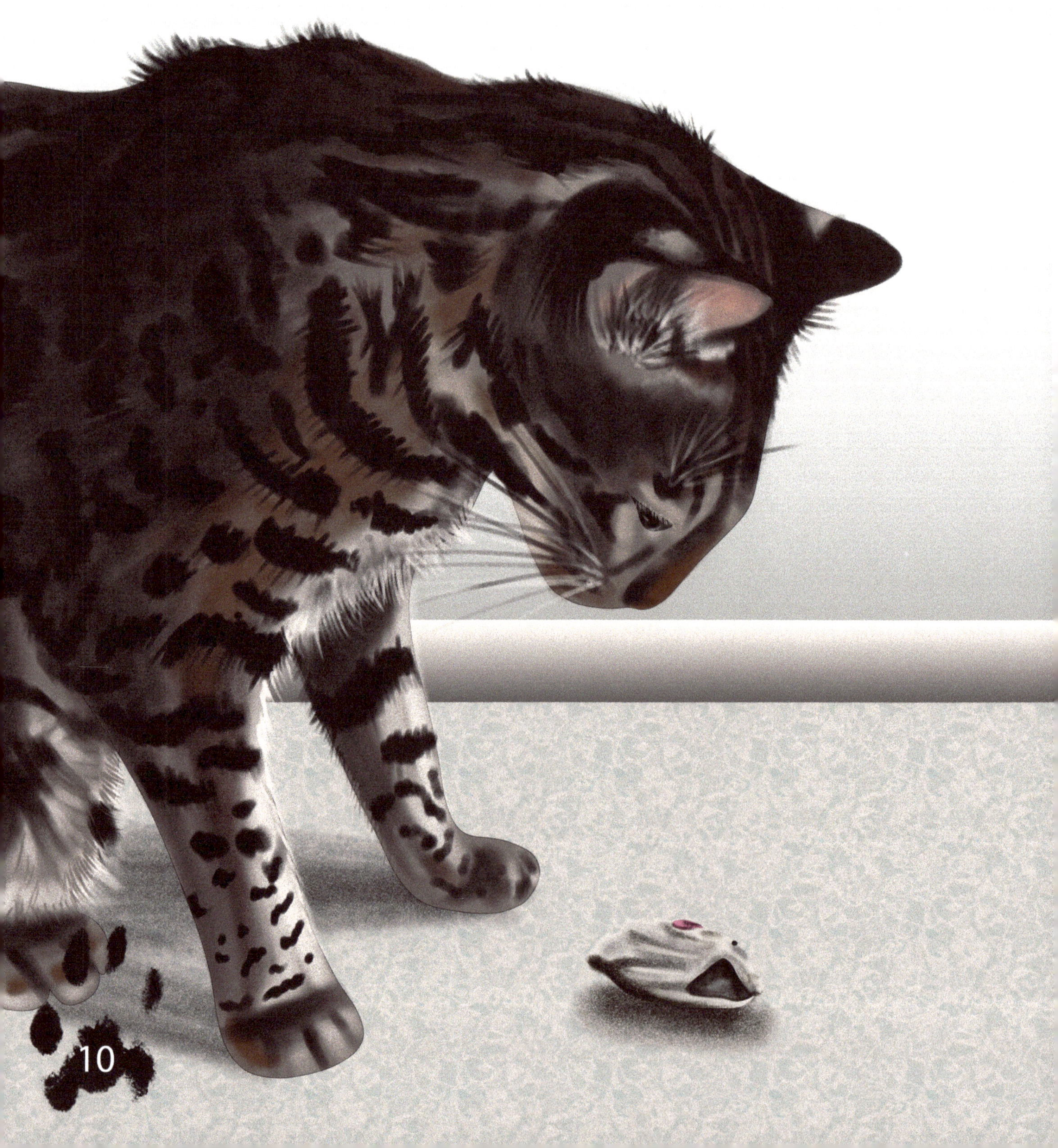

Ugh

Same Mouse Toy

Even though Mouse Toy was eating every day, his boo boo never got better. Maybe he needed something more than food to make him better.

Medicine
Mouse Toy Help

Flounder asked her mom to give Mouse Toy some medicine to help him feel better once and for all!

13

14

Mouse Toy Piano Now

Mouse Toy's medicine made him feel so much better. He could get back to his favorite activities with Flounder, like his daily piano lessons.

Ugh

Mouse Toy Christmas Tree All Done Yes Thank You

Mouse Toy tried to celebrate Christmas with a tiny Christmas tree. Flounder didn't want Mouse Toy to have a Christmas tree, so she told her mom to hide it from him. Mouse Toy's Jewish fans welcomed him into their community and now he celebrates Hanukkah with a tiny menorah instead.

Help Mouse Toy Want Tube Ride

After getting Christmas taken away from him, Mouse Toy decided he wanted a "tube ride", which is a fun activity that involves being spun around in Flounder's play tunnel by mom. Flounder joined him, of course.

19

20

Mouse Toy Water Yes

Because Mouse Toy lives such an active lifestyle since getting his medicine, it's important for him to drink a lot of water so he stays hydrated.

22

Mouse Toy was excited to go on a skateboard adventure with Flounder!

Adventure Yes Mouse Toy Excited Skateboard

24

Mouse Toy Beach More Swim

Mouse Toy's favorite thing to do, however, is swim at the beach with Flounder! They could swim all day!

Mouse Toy Rest

At the end of a
big day of adventures,
Mouse Toy needs to rest.

27

28

Love You Mouse Toy

29

To watch more videos of Flounder and Mouse Toy, be sure to follow them on social media:

@FlounderCat

@Flounder_Meatloaf

About the Author

Flounder is a remarkable cat who proudly calls herself a fish—a true Purrmaid at heart. She communicates with her family using Augmentative Interspecies Communication (AIC) buttons, which allow her to express her thoughts, feelings, and ideas in words. Through these buttons, Flounder discovered not only her voice, but also her talent for storytelling.

Her very first book is about her most favorite subject in the world: Mouse Toy, her beloved companion. Every word in this story comes directly from Flounder's button presses, making her the first cat to truly author a children's book.

Flounder's work is more than a sweet tale about a toy—it's a celebration of communication, imagination, and the unbreakable bonds between animals and their treasures. By sharing her story, Flounder reminds us that every being, no matter their species, has a voice worth listening to.

About the Illustrator

Nina Leipold, affectionately known as Flounder's mom, is an award-winning artist, animator, and children's book illustrator. Every illustration in this book was hand-drawn digitally with great care and attention to detail, capturing Flounder's unique personality and spirit. Nina's art brings Flounder's world to life, blending whimsy and heart in every page.

With deepest thanks to each contributor whose support helps weave a brighter, kinder world for all animals.

- Abbie Stahlin
- Abby Huhn
- Abigail Batchelder
- Adalynn Sickle
- Adriene Huffman
- Adryane Hansen
- Aleshia Trammel
- Alex Young
- Alice Friedman
- Alicia Barton
- Alise Scott
- Alison Lacasse
- Allie Ward
- Allyson Nedzbal
- Alyssa Fog
- Alyssa Fred Wong
- Amanda Austin Henderson
- Amanda Chowning
- Amanda Gann
- Amanda Martin
- Amanda Swan
- Amanda Webster
- Amber Fox
- Amelia Ignatovich
- Amelie Ya Deau
- Amy Luff Petry
- Amy Maguire
- Amy Reed
- Amy Sun
- Ana Delindro
- Anaïs Llodra
- Andrea Lilli
- Andrea Rieco
- Andrea Rodgers
- Andrea Savitch
- Andrea Stonebrook
- Andrea Wilson-Ewert
- Andrea Woodward
- Angie Cipolla
- Angela Dempster
- Angela Wise
- Anita Hall
- Anita Rohde
- Ann Hertenstein
- Ann Tiedeman
- Anna Hartwing
- Anna Luczak
- Anna Patricia Hawley
- Anna Zylinski
- Annemaree Winter
- Annette Sapiano
- April Bilbrey
- Arely Frias
- Arliss Paddock
- Ash, Smoke, Coal and Dracula Hill (and mom Dee)
- Ashley Running
- Aunt Beth Holden
- Aunt Kathy Focht
- Aunt Katlyn & Tio Roman
- Autumn Jensen
- Ava, the Black Dog
- Barbara Burns
- Barbara Noel
- Barbara Oehl
- Becky Czlapinski
- Becky Rooke
- Beth Poulter
- Billie Rewiri Lloyd
- BilliJoy Carson
- Birgitte Loizeau
- Björn Roslund
- Bo Mayo
- Bob & Linné Schulien
- Bonnie Littman
- Brad R. Nelson
- Brandi Spires
- Brandi-Amber Keenan
- Brandy Hartman
- Brett & Louanne Bertrand
- Brenda Mayo
- Brigitte Jean Förster
- Brionna Auriemma
- Brittany Box
- Britta Barnby
- Brooke A. Pry
- Brooke Parker
- Caitlin Golder
- Cara A. Mayo
- Carita Hauge
- Carina Löfkvist
- Carla Ballman
- Carla Voorhees
- Carol Folsom
- Carol Hawley
- Carol Ottersberg
- Carolann Gale
- Caroline Craig
- Carolyn Ferguson
- Carolyn Srite
- Carolyn Stewart-Childers
- Carrie (Emily & Lee) Wayne Mayo
- Cary Woods
- Cassandra Ankney
- Cath Ward
- Catherine Roebuck
- Cathy Kohansby
- Channie, Yoshi, Vixen, Mika, Kiki & Hachi
- Charlene Daigle
- Charlotte Heyns
- Chelleby Starr
- Cherie La Fleur
- Cheryl Fisher Bertrand
- Cheryl Rice
- Christie Boggs
- Christie Hayes
- Christie Meller
- Christina Biart
- Christina Pugh
- Christina Ruehmann
- Christine Aytug
- Christine Guzzetta
- Christine Kussey
- Christy Wain
- Christi Waters
- Cindy Palmer
- Citabria Gullett
- Claire Brennan-Jarrow
- Clifton Saliba
- Colleen England
- Corrine Holtrop
- Corrinne Vernick
- Crystal Wilvers
- Cydney Adler
- Cynsa Bonorris
- Cynthia Thrash
- Daniel Lysk
- Danielle Linton
- Dara Ishee
- Darleen Cahall
- Darlene Dempsey
- David Cox
- David Denny
- Deanna Robertson
- Deanne Biron
- Deborah Barry-Salazar
- Deborah Cole
- Deborah Engerman
- Deborah Highsmith
- Deborah Watson
- Debra Bauer

- Debra Eastman
- Debra Jones
- Deidre (Cam & Clio) Carovano
- Delahny Charbonneau
- Dena Fisher
- Dennise Marie Sullivan
- Denise Donahue
- Denise Isnor
- Deserae Nemeth
- Diana Garland
- Diana Romero
- Diana Sebastian
- Diane Dixon
- Diane Perry
- Disa-Lynne Momsen
- Donna Muldoon
- Donna Ortelli
- Donna Whalen
- Donna Wood
- Dorthy Ivester
- Dottie Faulkner
- E. Lily Lewis
- Edie Smith
- Effie Micheals
- Elaine Richardson
- Elise Liam
- Elizabeth Butler
- Elizabeth Marks
- Elizabeth Stephan
- Ellen Eades
- Elise Brandt
- Eloise Mehard
- Emily White
- Emily and Piper Williams
- Emma Burgar
- Emma Mazzocca
- Erika Vreeswijk
- Estie Kus
- Evi Verstraeten
- Felicity Clive
- Filaree Livezey
- Fiona Brown
- Fiona Strachan
- Frances Paquette
- Fred Wong
- Frederic Derouineau
- Gabi Beck
- Gail Cahill
- Gemma Janssen
- Gina C. Kleinleln
- Grace and Ava Neighbors
- Gwen Pinkerton
- Halee Eastin Brown
- Haley Sullivan
- Hannah Brotman
- Harlow M. Risinger
- Heather Blanarik
- Heather Collins
- Heather Flexer
- Heather Fryman
- Heidi Kelding
- Heather Kelley
- Heidi Lucille
- Heidi Maus
- Heidi Misener
- Hendrix Wilson
- Hilary Hopkins
- Hippi Starchild
- Ian Stewart
- Irene Koller
- Isa Swart
- Isabella Smalera Birns
- Iulia Moldovan
- J. Althaus
- Jadie Witteveen
- James Palmer Jr.
- James Vincent Hawley
- Jamie Hegarty
- Jamie Jones
- Jan Coleman
- Jan Smallwood
- JaNaye Bryson
- Jane Cox
- Jane Gaschler
- Janee Bussey
- Janet Fonoimoana
- Janet Koch
- Janice Elin
- Janita Lubbinge
- Janlyn Sinclair
- Jay KapLon
- Jean Hill
- Jeanette Ross
- Jeannie McCrary
- Jeanne Ruhl
- Jeffrey Niemi
- Jen Dunn
- Jenifer Wilson
- Jennifer Arthur
- Jennifer Berry
- Jennifer Cranch George
- Jennifer Davis
- Jennifer Kaplan
- Jennifer Rose McCauley
- Jenny Parke
- Jessica A. Paterson
- Jessica Shope
- Jessie Geivett
- Jill O'Meehan
- Joan Abele
- Joanna Panek
- JohnPaul Easton
- Joseph Dunn
- Joy Griffin
- Joyce Kent
- Julie Erickson
- Julie Guy
- Julie Heiple
- Julie McFadden
- Kaiden Alpert
- Kandra Swenson
- Karen Allen
- Karen Bickford
- Karen Doreen Garcia
- Karen Hyldgaard
- Karen Kidd
- Karen Potter-Witter
- Kari Eischens
- Kari Sullivan
- Karis Mohl
- Karla Hicks
- Karla Klingbell
- Katharina Achstetter
- Katherine Emilce Hawley
- Kathleen Conley
- Kathleen Cunningham
- Kathy Grube
- Kathy & Erin Hart
- Kathy Hawes
- Katie Giacomini
- Katie Morgan
- Kate Gentile
- Kate Siegel
- Kathryn Krohn
- Kelley Scott
- Kelly Alton
- Kelly Bloomfield
- Kelly Dearing
- Kelly F. Cunningham
- Kelly, human Mom of Odin & Frankie
- Kelly Komisor
- Kelly Pollock
- Kelly Shock
- Kellsey Schaffer
- Kenna Bjerstedt
- Kenzie Hulley
- Kerrilee Wong
- Kim Pietruszewski
- Kim Valente
- Kimberli Gerlach
- Kimberly Roberts
- Kimberly Skrinak
- Kimberly Tribo
- Kindra Cihocki
- Kityn Mitchell
- Kona Lopez
- Kristin Bedont-Combs
- Kristen Castracane
- Kristen Morgan-May
- Kristin Jacobsen
- Kristina Adkins
- Kristina Jose

- Kristine Roberts
- Kristine Sihto
- Kyla & Kala Tomlin
- Kymberly Irons
- Laina Christner
- Laila Bailey
- Larry Atcheson & Willow
- Larry Brannan
- Lauren DeLand
- Lauren Griffith & Walker
- Lauren Thompson
- Lauri Campbell
- Laurie Reid
- Leah Brown
- Leana Varnhagen
- Leanne Dillian
- Leeann Hughes
- Leina Cooper
- Leslie Farrow
- Leslie Kimberly
- Lesley Olson
- Leticia Zarco
- Liana LaCroix
- Libby White
- Lilith Fuller
- Lily Jungnickel
- Linda Bowman
- Linda Daugherty
- Linda Rasp
- Ling Huang
- Lisa Benson
- Lisa Chipp
- Lisa Domigan
- Lisa Estus
- Lisa Goodell
- Lisa Lunsford
- Lisa Marchitello
- Lisa Neal
- Lisa Nolan
- Lisa Schleicher
- Lora Andrews
- Lora Vencill
- Lora Weems
- Lorena Estrada
- Lori Bailey
- Lori Darnall
- Lori Angelica Gibson
- Loryn Tashima
- Lynn Adams
- Lynn Barnard
- Lynn Browder
- Marcy Rogers
- Margaret Jenny
- Mari Ono
- Maria Capili
- Maria Micks
- Marisha Steen
- Marion McDowell
- Marion Soechtig
- Marjoleine Leclerc
- Marla Martinez
- Mario Rivas
- Marti McBride
- Mary Harrison
- Mary Kidwell
- Mary Mattiaccci
- Mary Meredith
- Mary Yakibchuk
- Matilda Kiteborg
- Mayme Eilers
- Megan Elsig
- Megan Goulding
- Megan McKeon
- Melanie Hermann
- Melinda Schroeder
- Melissa Bassil
- Melissa & Harrison Gebel
- Melissa Knecht
- Melissa Mead
- Melissa Rosas
- Meowamine
- Michaela Elaine
- Michele Welch
- Michelle Boonzaier
- Michelle Mulford
- Michelle Wood
- Mimi Keeler
- Misty Moo McCreanor
- Monique Yanez
- Morgane Heyse
- Nancy Linkesh
- Nancy Merchant
- Nancy Milam
- Nancy Oswald
- Naomi Turnley
- @NatsRallyCat
- Nicole Blanchette
- Nicole Corbett
- Nicole Hawkey
- Nicole Sequiera
- Nicole Shay
- Nicki Goodman
- Niko Brown
- Nina Saulic
- Ning Chua
- Nurde Yufya
- Oli, Minnie, Gizzy, Geisha (& Mum Alissa)
- Olivia Saunterzoff
- Paige Anderson
- Pamela Erinakis
- Pamela Andersen
- Pamela Hodges
- Pamela Kovach
- Pamela Stone
- Pamela Sumler
- Patricia Bowen
- Patricia Middlemiss
- Patricia Taylor
- Patrick Young
- Paula Mader Brensinger
- Paula (& Rho) Schroeder
- Paxton Richmond
- Pearson-Moore Family
- Peggy Coronado
- Peggy Howland
- Peggy PawPaw Walch
- Pip Broughton
- Piper Huffman
- Pravah Jayaprakash
- Princess Petrie Potato Soup Kitten
- Rachel & Mitchell Hughes
- Rachel Taber-Hamilton
- Randee Bulla
- Raquel Engelke
- Rebecca Calhoun
- Rebecka Johansson
- Rene Latham
- Rhonda Dredden Lancaster
- Rhonda Fleming
- Rie Nagami
- RJ Pettaway
- Robin Schneider
- Ronan Willoughby
- Roxanne Gullett
- Rue Ann Jones
- Ruth Fletcher Gage
- Ruth Vaughn
- Ryan Donovan
- Sabine Naudier
- Sally Kiehnau
- Samantha Mahoney
- Sandra del Tiempo
- Sandra Geden
- Sandra Sepulveda
- Sandra Tiffin
- Sandy Sagneri
- Sarah Conway
- Sarah Westling
- Saralyn Hubbard
- Scherra Bartoli
- Seth Laff
- Severina Fabros
- Shanna & Alissa Walker
- Shane Brandes
- Shanrae'l Murphy
- Shanna Brown
- Shannon Taylor
- Sharon Lai
- Sharon Sweeney

- Shawn Tennant
- Shawnmarie Berry
- Sheila Cook
- Sherry Ramaila
- Shirley Thompson
- Sif and Sølv
- Sienna Runge
- Silus & Socorro De Hoyos
- Sir Toe Beans
- Social4Society
- Sonja Hofmann
- Sonya Kunkle
- Sophie Bratton
- Stacey Lanzillotta
- Staffan Näs
- Stephanie Shankle
- Stephen Horan
- Sue Kenworthy
- Suehan Estrada
- Susan Curley
- Susan Davy
- Susan Fitzpatrick
- Susan Goodman
- Susan Hailman
- Susan J Wright
- Susan Keays
- Susan Knisley
- Susan Nichols
- Susanne Horvat
- Suzan Bailey
- Suzanne Melton
- Sylvia Owen
- Tamara Dominguez
- Tamara Norton
- Teddy
- Teresa Crawford
- Teresa Martignetti
- Teresa Williams
- Tess Fisher
- The Budnicks
- The Vandergrants
- Thomas Jungnickel
- Tim Howe
- Tina Dial
- Tina Gordon
- Tina Hoag
- Tina Marie
- Tina Steed
- Tinna Helgadóttir
- Tina Batchelder
- Tobi Lenker
- Tom Ripp
- Tonia Burley
- Tonia Martin
- Tonya Jones
- Tracey Gendron
- Tracey Taylor
- Tracie W. Denga
- Tracy Sharp
- Tristan & Hendrix Holden
- Tyler Harms
- Valerie Huss
- Veronica Stanley
- Vicki DiPietro
- Violet Folsom
- Virginia Conterato
- Vivian Hance
- Wendy Clark
- Wendy Darling
- Wendy Donovan, Adventure Cat
- Wendy Gronemeyer
- Wendy Kohnenkamp
- Wesley Jackson
- Weston Runge
- WysPurr & PepPurr Carter Shore
- Yumiko Mikanagi
- Yvette Fenning
- Yvonne Pona
- Yvonne Russo-Devosa
- Zayn Beauregard-Shah
- Zia Moon
- Zo and Vania Hawkins

o learn how to teach your pet to use buttons, please visit: Floundercat.com/Buttons

Join FlounderLand!

Visit our website to check out our online store and to join our FlounderLand Community – gain access to never before seen Flounder content, training tips, discounts, and more!

All Merch designs hand drawn by Nina

www.ingramcontent.com/pod-product-compliance
Lightning Source LLC
LaVergne TN
LVHW070122091125
824940LV00004B/15